This book belongs

For Joe - K.R.
For Premmi - A.N.

Bertie The Balloon at the Zoo first published by Kim Robinson and Aneta Neuman
This edition published 2016
Text copyright © Kim Robinson 2009
Illustrations © Aneta Neuman 2015

Printed in Poland
ISBN 978-0-9934627-1-9

www.bertietheballoon.com
Bertietheballoon@hotmail.com

Written by

Kim Robinson

Illustrated by

Aneta Neuman

Bertie The Balloon at the Zoo

Bertie is a **BIG**, red, shiny balloon.
He's round, squishy and shaped like
the **MOON**.

Bertie can fly high up in the sky,
Higher than the trees -
oh MY, oh MY!

How lucky that he is so light and free
As balloons are filled with air, you see.

yyyyh.

But, be careful Bertie, don't get swept awayyyyh.
The wind's a dangerous place
for you to play.

Bertie has a secret he wants to share with you.
Not only does he fly, but he can talk, too!

For Bertie is a M★A★G★I★C★A★L★ balloon
Who goes on adventures,
as you'll see soon.

Bertie belongs to a boy called Hugh
And today they are going on a trip to the Zoo.

Hugh holds Bertie by a **long** piece of lace,
Tied tightly around his wrist, just in case!

Into the car, and they're on their way.
Another exciting day ahead, hip, hip,
hoOray!

Bertie wonders what animals he'll see,
An elephant, a tiger, or maybe a chimpanzee?

"Where shall we start?" asks Bertie with a smile.
"I know," said Hugh.
"I want to see a crocodile."

So, off they went in search of the crocs
Past tigers, snakes, lizards and peacocks.

"There are the crocs," shouted Hugh, full of glee.
"What BIG teeth," he laughed.
"They could easily eat me!"

"Hold me tight," Bertie whimpered. "Don't let me go."
But just as he said it, the wind started to blow.

The sun disappeared and the clouds turned grey.
"Oh no," said Bertie. "It's turning into a windy day."

The wind grew stronger and the rain fell fast.
Bertie got squashed as everyone rushed past.

As Hugh ran for cover he saw a bolt of lightning.
He turned to Bertie, "Golly gosh, that
was
frightening!"

But there was no balloon,
just a damp piece of lace.

Bertie had disappeared, gone without a trace.

Desperately, Hugh looked all around,
But poor Bertie was nowhere to be found.

"Where are you?"

cried Hugh full of despair.
But poor Bertie was already

flying away
in the air.

With his eyes shut tight, the balloon soared on
Over huts and cages just
blowing on and on.

Bertie took a deep breath and opened one eye
"I'm all alone," he cried, letting out a
HUGE sigh.

He flew over giraffes with very long necks.
He sailed over zebras with stripes but no checks.

He saw alligators and lions with very sharp claws.

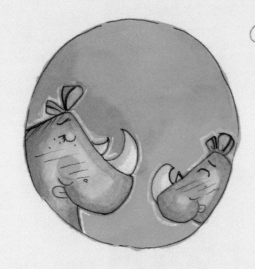

He spied rhinos and bears with GIGANTIC paws.

All of a sudden Bertie was blown into a cage.
The balloon spied a tiger, his face full of rage.

"This isn't good," Bertie said, shaking with fear.
"Quick. Think," Bertie told himself.

"I need to GET OUT
of here."

Just as the tiger was about to pounce,
Bertie puffed up his chest and got ready to
bOuNcE.

He bent his string and crouched closer to the floor.
He had to act quickly to escape the tiger's claw.

As the beast ran towards him, Bertie sprang
into the sky.
Luckily the breeze caught him and
lifted him up high.

The angry tiger jumped up, swiping the air,
But only Bertie's string was in reach and it
tickled his ear!

Safe once again,
Bertie took in his view
Of all the animals
who lived in the zoo.

Then in the distance
he spied some monkeys
Eating bananas, doing somersaults
and swinging in trees.

The wind slowed down as
Bertie flew near,
But he wasn't worried;
the monkeys looked
full of cheer.

Lower and lower he sailed
towards their dwelling
And with one last gust
of wind he was there,
he was IN!

"Hello, happy monkey," Bertie cheerfully said.
Confused, the monkey just scratched his head.

"A new ball," shouted the smallest of the bunch
And with that, he gave an almighty **PUNCH**.

"Ouch," shouted Bertie. "I'm not a toy!"
But the monkeys didn't stop,
they just screamed with joy.

Louder and louder

the monkeys joked and jeered,
Hitting the balloon
harder and faster as they cheered.

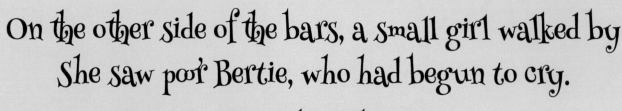

On the other side of the bars, a small girl walked by
She saw poor Bertie, who had begun to cry.

"Don't hurt him,"
she SCREAMED with all her might.
The monkeys stopped; she'd given them a fright.

"Give him to me now," she told the ringleader.
"Otherwise you'll go without tea
as I'll tell your feeder."
Worried, the monkey moved closer to the girl
And with one last hit, Bertie, he did hurl.

He whooshed over the bars, his head spinning around
Straight into her arms, safe and sound.

"Hello, Mr Balloon, you can stay with me."
"Thank you," said Bertie, his face full of glee.

"My name is May and I live on a farm."
"That sounds fun," smiled Bertie, feeling calm.
Now safe and secure with his brand new mate.
"It's time for a new ADVENTURE,"
Bertie cheered. "And I can't wait!"

THE END

Look out for more
Bertie The Balloon
adventures coming soon!

Printed in Great Britain
by Amazon